Call In Well

Timothy Orley

AuthorHouse™
1663 Liberty Drive
Bloomington, IN 47403
www.authorhouse.com
Phone: 1 (800) 839-8640

Published by AuthorHouse 07/06/2018

ISBN: 978-1-5462-3174-5 (sc)
ISBN: 978-1-5462-3173-8 (e)

Library of Congress Control Number: 2018902845

Print information available on the last page.

author HOUSE®

For all of the nice people I've met along the way.

Open this book if you dare.
Open this book but beware.

For this book may take you to faraway places,
Where you may meet people with faraway faces.
You'll see how they live, how they work, how they walk,
How they greet when they meet, what they eat, how they talk.

There are times when this book may be very intense.
There are times when this book might not make any sense.
You may laugh, you may dance, you may sing, you may smile,
So take off your shoes, and please stay for a while.

Open this book if you dare,
For I have some stories to share.

Come in.
Come in.

Big Betty's Pizza

Big Betty's Pizza is right down the street,
And she'll make you a pizza that's never been beat.

Just ask for Betty; she wears a blue bonnet.
And ask her to fix one with *everything* on it.

She'll start with some cheese and some sauce and some dough,
But this is just the beginning, you know—

An onion, an olive, a mushroom or three,
One pickle, one pepper, and one little pea.

Betty may then add the odd piece of candy,
Which to sweeten the pizza will come in quite handy—
A cookie or two straight from the box,
A new magic marker and six sweaty socks,

A baseball, a football, a left-footed shoe,
A pencil, a cupcake, a copper kazoo.

She'll add a marshmallow and one piece of toast,
But that is not all, not even almost—

A backpack, a snack pack, a rock, and a rake,
A pot, and a pail, and a snail, and a snake,

A new suit, a grapefruit, a clock that tells time,
One ruble, one peso, one dollar, one dime,

An acorn, a french horn, a belt, and a boat,
A fan, and a pan, and a can, and a coat,

Some old reading glasses and a warm winter glove,
All mixed with molasses and made well with love.

Just ask for Betty; she wears a blue bonnet.
And ask her to fix one with *everything* on it.

A little too much? Just ask for Jane.
And Jane will be happy to make you a plain.

The Wee Pirates

We the Wee Pirates of the Big Backyard Bluff
Are teeny and tiny but terribly tough.
We'll sing pirate songs as we steal all your stuff,
We the Wee Pirates of the Big Backyard Bluff.

We may say, "Ahoy there, me matey" or "Arrrrrrrr,"
"Shiver me timber" or "Hardee har har."
We'll chase down your ship wherever you are
And plunder the gold from your treasure chest jar.

We may walk with a limp when the weather's no good
Because of a leg which is made out of wood.
And a parrot which is easily misunderstood
Will squawk dirty words as he sits where he should.

Our story will be legend and one you should tell
And share with your friends and learn very well.
We the Wee Pirates cannot possibly fail.
Now all we must do...

Is learn how to sail.

Call In Well

I didn't go to work today.
I wasn't sick or ill.
I simply called my boss to say
I'm feeling way too well.

I hopped right out of bed instead
And set about my way,
Very pleased and pleasantly
Preparing for my day.

I went downstairs for breakfast,
Chocolate milk and cake,
Which is of course my favorite meal
To eat after I wake.

I put my shoes and socks on,
And I headed out the door–
A very merry world for me
To see and to explore.

I went over to the park
And had a walk along the lake,
Looking at the ducks and fish
And even at a snake.

I do not like to look at snakes,
But today it seemed okay.
We greeted one another
And then continued on our way.

And then a thought occurred to me,
As thoughts they sometimes do,
The more friendly that you are to snakes,
The more friendly they to you.

I walked along a little more
Through the flowers and the trees,
Looking at the butterflies, the blue birds,
And the bees.

I was having quite a day,
But I hadn't had my fill.
I could not have gone to work today–
I simply felt too well.

Oh, what a view! The sky was blue;
The puffy clouds were white.
The sun was out and all about
And shining very bright.

I carried on down the road
To the city square,
Where people like to meet and greet
And walk and talk and share.

I made a few new friends,
Some were young and some were old.
We talked and laughed and learned
From all the stories that we told.

Everyone was happy,
As far as I could tell.
I could not have gone to work today—
I simply felt too well.

I left the square and carried on
Down the road a while,
Looking all around me
And continuing to smile.

I skipped, I hopped, I flipped, I flopped
And did other things I like.
I ran along. I sang a song.
I had a happy hike.

I strolled right through the meadow
And got lost along the sea.
But lost or found, I was bound
For where I was meant to be.

From here to there and back again,
I left quite a trail.
I could not have gone to work today–
I simply felt too well.

I was having an adventure.
My day was going great.
But it was time to go back home,
As it was getting late.

I made myself some supper
And ate ice cream after that.
I put on my pajamas,
And I sat down with my cat.

I thought about my day,
With a smile on my face.
I thought about the wonderful way
I went from place to place.

I took my favorite book;
I skimmed a bit and read.
I fell asleep, while counting sheep,
Upon my cozy bed.

Now,
Before you fall asleep,
Think of the ways which you have fun.
Don't be afraid to dance and shout
And skip about and run.

Go have an adventure.
Create a story you can tell.
And remember, sometimes you cannot work—

Sometimes you feel too well.

Eksilent Studint

I am an eksilent studint,
And I go to skool every day.
I'm quiet and nice. I take good advice
And lissen to what my teechers say.

I always finnish my homework.
I get into line, and I wate.
I put up my hand when I don't undirstand,
And for clastime I nevr am late.

I only have one vary small problem.
I don't know if you are able to till.
I am an eksilent studint,
But I'm told I must learn how to spill.

I Woke Up Late

I woke up late for school today. I jumped right out of bed.
I ran across the floor and tripped and landed on my head.

I got dressed so quickly,
I didn't get it right.
I put my clothes on backward;
It was not a pretty sight.

I ran downstairs.
I grabbed my bag.
There was no time to eat.

I sat down in the hall
And put my shoes
On the wrong feet.

This made it very hard to run
To the bus stop, I would say,
Because my feet and shoes
Were going in a different way.

When I finally arrived,
I saw the bus had gone,
And this simply was not good,
As the bus I was not on.

I had to walk to school today
And make my teacher wait.
And now I know, wherever I go,
I shouldn't wake up late.

My Boat

This is my boat.
My boat can float.
My boat is a nice place to be.

But if my boat
Were unable to float,
I would get to see more of the sea.

Another Me

I really wish that there could be
A very useful second me–

A me who could help out with all of my chores
And clean up, and sweep up, and mop up my floors.

A me to do dishes after I dine–
A me such as this would be really fine.

A me to do homework when I want to rest–
A me such as this would be just the best.

A me to fold laundry and take out the trash,
A me to buy candy when I run out of cash,

A nice me to walk with and talk with and play,
A nice me to speak with and spend time each day–

Alas, I know there is only one me,
And I will probably not find another.
But I have the next best thing there could be–
I have a nice older brother.

Ben Backward

Ben Backward is name my, hi.
Backwardville from am I.

Different is town my see.
Way this talk and walk we.

All at me understand you do?
To hard very try should you.

Carefully study, and book a get.
Easier become will it.

Think I, become will we friends good,
Me like speak to learn you should.

Me like just backward be to try.
Bye bye–soon you see will I.

Homework

I didn't do my homework.
My teacher asked me why.
"And please tell me the truth," she said.
"You know it's wrong to lie."

This made things rather tricky,
As my plan was to deceive
And make up a good story that
She might just best believe.

I was going to tell my teacher I was working in my room,
When suddenly I heard out back, a very scary boom.

So I looked out the window to the big boom down below,
And when the smoke began to clear, I saw a UFO.

A silver ship with flashing lights sat there on the lawn,
And aliens with purple tights danced around till dawn.

Then they took my homework I was working on for school;
They used it and my pencil for their UFO ship fuel.

Their ship took off; it lifted and headed toward the sky.
But I couldn't tell this story,
Because...

I know it's wrong to lie.

I was going to tell my teacher that my work was in my pack,
And when I left my home today, my pack was on my back.

I was walking down the road to go to school to learn,
But then for some odd reason, I made quite a wrong turn.

I walked on a while 'til my feet began to tire,
When suddenly I came across a brightly burning fire.

And round about the fire were several silly folks,
Who chanted a weird language and wore pink polka-dotted cloaks.

They took my pack right off my back, which I used at school for learning,
And threw my homework in the fire—I guess to keep it burning.

The fire burned on steadily, rising up so high,
But I couldn't tell this story
Because...

I know it's wrong to lie.

I was going to tell my teacher I was walking down the road,
When I came across a terrifying, tiny talking toad.

He called me names, he burped a bit, he liked to taunt and tease me.
And he said, "Give me your homework, and do your best not to displease me."

When I asked him why, he said, "You do not need to know.
Just give me your homework, and then quickly turn and go."

And then that toad, it hopped away with my homework and a fly.
But I couldn't tell this story
Because...

I know it's wrong to lie.

I had so many stories.
I had so many tales
Of ghosts and goblins, unicorns,
Of pirate ships and whales.

I had so many stories
And tales that I created,
But because I know it's wrong to lie,

I told my teacher my dog ate it.

Believe It or Not

Becca believes blue elephants are right outside her door.
Theo thinks three monsters live beneath his floor.
Connor has a closet goblin.
Erin has an elf.
Franny's fancy fairies spend their evenings on her shelf.

Werewolves roam in Bill's backyard at nighttime, when it's dark,
And down the street a little ways is Patty's pixie park.

Nancy knows her lucky shirt will help her ace the test.
Nathan knows his lucky shoes will help him race his best.

Sarah says that six is good,
But her brother Chuck
Prefers the number seven,
Saying six will bring bad luck.

I believe in what I see.
I think this is enough.
But I am still good friends with those
Who believe in other stuff.

Everyone thinks differently
About what is real and true.
What may be true for someone else
May not be true for you.

Cooties

I've had a belly ache or two,
A sniffle and a sneeze.
I've had a fever and a flu.
Oh, jeez! Oh, jeez! Oh, jeez!

I've stubbed a finger and a toe.
I've had a cackle and a cough.
My nose has run both fast and slow.
My fingernail fell off.

I've been hit by several stones.
I've clanged and banged my head.
I've bammed and boomed and bumped my bones.
I've fallen out of bed.

I've hurt my eye.
I've hurt my chin.
I've hurt my thigh.
I've hurt my shin.

I've been through every kind of sick,
And injuries, please take your pick.

But yesterday I did endure
A strange disease I could not cure.

For yesterday, I'm sad to say, when I met Catherine Cuties,
She went and passed along to me a severe case of the cooties!

Good News

I watched the news the other day,
And everything was bad.
Crying, fighting everywhere–
It made me really sad.

I turned my TV off,
So I couldn't hear them talk.
I turned my TV off,
And I went out for a walk.

And this is what I saw:

A child who was really sweet,
Helped a lady cross the street;

A man who didn't wait at all
To help a boy after a fall;

A lady picking up some trash and cleaning up the street;
A little boy with his dog, feeding him a treat;

A daughter and her daddy were walking hand in hand;
A mother and her baby boy were learning how to stand.

Good people and good news were everywhere around.
Good people and good news were all throughout my town.

More Me

The me that you see
Is just not enough.
If I had more me,
I could do much more stuff.

Four eyes, for example, would be just the best–
Two eyes to read with and two eyes to rest.
I would have pleasant dreams and prepare for my test.
Four eyes, for example, would be just the best.

Of course, I'd be happy with one extra nose,
To follow the fragrance wherever it goes.
Some perfume, some popcorn, a radiant rose
Would smell even better with one extra nose.

An ear on the back of my head would be fine.
I could hear danger coming right up from behind.
It may look quite silly, but I wouldn't mind.
An ear on the back of my head would be fine.

And when dining away on a fine fancy feast,
One mouth is too few; I would like two at least.
I could dine well on food from the furthest Far East.
One mouth is too few; I would like two at least.

A few extra hands would be quite a sight–
Maybe three on the left and four on the right.
I would use them to shake with while flying a kite,
And an arm for each hand would make it quite right.

Two legs and two feet are okay but not great.
Two legs and two feet are not as great as eight.
They would help me move quicker, so I'd never be late
To meet with my friends or take out a date.

Yes,
These simple things would be okay to change,
But I won't overdo it–

I don't want to look strange.

My Very Own Language

Some people speak English.
Some people speak Greek
Japanese, Chinese, or Dutch.

Some people speak Irish, Icelandic, Italian,
Flemish, French, Finnish, and such.

As nice as these are,
They're too many by far
To learn and get into my head.
So rather than learn,
I thought I'd have a turn
And make up my own language instead.

"Tinker ma slink" is "How do you do?"
And "Dink dink" of course is just "Hi."
"Awilla ma wink" is "I'm fine. How are you?"
"A tink tinka link" is "Goodbye."

"Hibby" is "red" and "dibby" is "blue,"
And "hibbymadibby" is "purple."
"Tik, Tak, atown" is "green, pink, and brown,"
And "yellow" is "murpolly wurple."

"One, two, three, four" is "bing, bang, boom, boor,"
And the number "five" is "kladumple."
"Six, seven, eight" is "scip, dippy, date."
"Nine" is "hoopwoop," and "ten" is "flamumple."

For breakfast, you might eat some "toppidy snops,"
Which tastes great when you dip it in "sqimple,"
For lunch, you should try "nop bolly wops,"
With a cup of delicious, cool "timple."
In the evening sit down at the "wumpet,"
And dine well on "serzy magoo."
Then if you're still a bit "pumpet,"
Just add on some "sliptippy" too.

Your "mom" is a "mimi."
Your "dad" is a "spid."
Your "brother's" a "didi."
Your "sister's" a "krid."
Your "dog" is a "twappy."
Your "cat" is a "twim."
And you'll all be happy
At home in your "nim."

And you may wear a "nerdle" or a "nic nodder pot,"
Depending on whether the weather is hot.
And if it is not, then you might want to wear
A "hoppedy clop" and "boppedy bair."

There are many more words in my language to go,
So I made a short list of some you should know.

Herpa ma vert,
Nop flock hocktoodle,
Sim sim malim,
Kicky kapoodle,
Lickady, Stickady, Stunky magoo,
Hickady, Dickady, Crickady koo,
Wumpidy slump, Timm wizady snizz,
Pimpammy, Ramtammy, Timtammer tiz
Hippidy, Skippidy, Tickidy tee,
Huppity, Muppity, Snuppity snee

So, please, practice hard, and learn a few words.
You can study the book on the shelf.
And should you learn to say a few words,
I won't have to speak to myself.

Sleep

I can sleep through thunderstorms,
The raining and the pouring.
I can sleep through math class,
When my teacher is too boring.

I can sleep when mother says,
"It's time to rise and shine."
And when my alarm clock tries to wake me up,
I seem to sleep just fine.

I can sleep on beds, of course,
And sofas and on chairs.
I can even sleep at tables
And while lying down on stairs.

I sleep well at night outside,
Underneath the stars.
I sleep well on planes and trains
And bicycles and cars.

I sleep very well when sitting down.
I can sleep while standing up.
I sleep well while eating dinner
And when drinking from my cup.

I am so good at sleeping.
I can even sleep while walking.
And although I might not make much sense,
I often sleep while talking.

I can sleep through thunderstorms,
The raining and the pouring.
The only thing I can't sleep through
Is my brother's snoring!

51

Dear Santa

Dear Santa, here's my Christmas list
Of things that I would like:

A private plane,
A rocket train,
And a flying bike.

A chocolate bed to rest my head might be kind of cool.
And if it isn't too much trouble, could you please shut down my school?

Santa, I don't want to ride on buses anymore;
That's why I'll need a greenish-purple, pink pet dinosaur.
I'll ride him, and I'll feed him as we're going down the street,
Waving to my friends and all the people we would meet.

And if you could make me really, really, really, really tall,
Then they wouldn't pick me last when it's time for basketball.

Of course, I want a castle and a dragon and a moat,
A roller coaster and perhaps a helicopter boat,

A magic wand, a magic pond
Filled with magic fish
That swim around and greet me
As they grant my every wish.

Santa, here's my Christmas list.
I know it may be tough,
So just keep my family safe and warm,
And this will be enough.

My New Friend

I'm having a bit of a problem.
I have only myself to blame.
I made a new friend yesterday,
But I cannot remember his name.

Was it Adam or Abe,
Benjamin, Babe,
Billy Bob, Bo, Buck, or Brad?
Was it Charlie or Chauncy or Chandler or Chancy or Chippy or Chappy or Chad?

It wasn't David, Don, Dallas, or Derrick,
Nor was it Ed, Eddy, Ernie, or Eric.

I don't think it was Frank.
I don't think it was Gary
Or Henry, Hank, Hannibal, Hugo, or Harry.

Ian and Irwin surely won't do,
Nor will Joe, John,
Kip, Kenny, or
Larry, Lee, Lou.

And I'm fairly certain that it didn't sound like
Maddux, Max, Malakai, Marco, or Mike,
Nathan, Nick, Noah,
Nor Owen, Orion,
Peter, Paul, Patrick,
Quinn, Quincy,
Rob, Ryan.

It wasn't Sam,
Tim, Tom, Tony, or Troy.
I just can't remember the name of that boy.

Ulysses and Ulrich are not even close,
Nor are Victor, Van Vincent, Van Vijay, Van Vose.

It wasn't Walker, Will, Willy, or Wayne,
Xavier, Xander,
York, Yogie,
Or Zane.

I just can't remember his name to no end—
That's the last time I make an imaginary friend.

59

The Not-So-Super Heroes

We are not perfect tens.
We're not exactly zeros.
We are the best of friends,
The Not-So-Super Heroes!

We may not save the world today,
And I'll tell you why:
We are not strong or brave; in fact,
We cannot even fly.

So let me introduce you to our not-so-super crew,
And tell you all about the not-so-super things we do.

The first member of our baffling band
Can't help but speak in rhyme,
Which you may find confusing
If with him you spend some time.

He might say, "Jello chair.
Jello chair. Cow car blue?
I pope bat bee become wood ends
And talk to weather to."

Sir Rhyme-a-Lot will rhyme it up the very best he can,
And this is the first member of our not-so-super clan.

The next member of our group
To wear the not-so-super crown
Is a man from faraway,
Who is unable to sit down.

He cannot sit when eating
Or when watching the TV.
He cannot sit when sleeping
Or when sailing on the sea.
He cannot sit when driving
Or when riding on his bike.
He cannot sit when tired
After going on a hike.

Captain Cannot Sit Down
Will go through shoes galore,
And Captain Cannot Sit Down
Will stand forever more.

For the third member of our team,
I hope that you can wait,
Because this member, it would seem,
Is always very late.

She is late for everything.
She just can't get in gear.
In fact, she missed her birthday once
By more than half a year.

For being late, there's no debate
That she is the winner.
She wakes up each and every day
And starts by eating dinner.

Lady Late is very nice
And very cute and clever,
But you'll have to take my word,
As she may not show up ever.

Have you met Mr. Opposite?
Well, you will today.
He does things just like you or I,
But not in the same way.

He wakes up every evening,
And he goes to bed at dawn.
He does exercise when tired,
And when wide awake, he'll yawn.

He'll put his shoes right on his hands;
His gloves go on his feet.
He says "Hello" when leaving
And "Goodbye" to meet and greet.

Should you meet Mr. Opposite,
And do not know what to say,
Just speak sort of normally,
But not in the same way.

The fifth and final member of our not-so-super scene
Is me–
A girl who really, really loves the color green!

I live in a green house
In the middle of Green Street.
I like to wear green skirts
And put green shoes upon my feet.

I sit on my green sofa
As I watch my green TV,
Eating a green apple,
While sipping hot green tea.

My floor is green. My door is green.
My cat and dog are too.
I have no time for purple, yellow,
Red, or black, or blue.

For the Girl of Green the color's green,
No matter what the season,
And please don't ask me why, because
I don't think there's a reason.

69

We are not perfect tens.
We're not exactly zeros.
We are the best of friends,
The Not-So-Super Heroes.

Now,
Maybe if you practice the not-so-super things you do,
The next member of our not-so-super crew might just be you!

When I'm a Ghost

I don't go to the attic when my older brother dares me.
I just stay downstairs and hide.
I don't go to the attic because the ghost there often scares me,
And I don't want to be stuck inside.

The moaning and the groaning and the clanging and the banging
Make me run and scream and shout.
The moaning and the groaning and the clanging and the banging
Are noises I can do without.

And I often think that one day should I become a ghost,
I won't be very scary, but I'll be a happy host.

I will just say, "Welcome. Welcome how do you do?"
And I won't moan or groan about or clang or bang or boo.

Kind

I think you will find
If you are kind,
People are kinder to you.

So take my advice
And try to be nice,
In all of the things that you do.

CPSIA information can be obtained
at www.ICGtesting.com
Printed in the USA
BVHW02s2032200718
522178BV00020B/321/P

9 781546 231745